# Tinker's Christmas

By

**Sandra Jones Cropsey**

**Illustrations**

By

**Barbra K. Mudd**

**Wright Books**
Fayetteville, Ca.

Library of Congress Cataloging-in-Publication Data'
Sandra Jones Cropsey


Tinker's Christmas
Sandra Jones Cropsey – 1st ed.
Case Bound   cm.
ISBN: 0-9652368-8-9 (tr)


1.  Children's book, Christmas theme, Moral story / United States
2.  Tinker's Adventures at Christmas time.


Printed in Hong Kong


First Edition

1 2 3 4 5 6 7 8 9 10

Book Design and Illustrations by Barbra K. Mudd


WRIGHT BOOKS
Fayetteville, Ga.

*My Thanks*

*For all the wonderful people who believed in me and whose love and kindness has made the world a nicer place.*

*For my husband, Paul, and our two boys, Justin and Brad, whose love and support helped get my train up in the sky.*

*For a truly fantastic editor, Lydia Griffin.*

*For my sisters and brother—Shirley, Stanley and Shelby—and our good and loving parents—Hugh and Ora Jones. A special thanks to my sister, Shirley, who has always taken care of me more often like a mother than a sister and a special thanks to her zany sidekick, Marvin. And for my sister-in-law, Jeanette and my brother-in-law, Johnny, and all our truly remarkable nieces and nephews. And finally for our newest additions—Emmie and Jake Harrod, who make life sweet.*

*For our dear Mom—Katherine Cropsey—a warm and loving treasure. And for Pat and Sue Troy and Tony and Kathy Panella and even more terrific nieces and nephews.*

*For my best and most needed agent, Reverend Bruce Morgan, whose spiritual guidance has helped sustain so many of us through the difficult times.*

*For my writing buddies--Joy Barrett, Jean Ann Hancher, Lisa Arnold and Dale Davis Murphy—who shored me up when it looked like my train might not take off.*

*For Mr. Warren Frye, who so generously shared his love of trains.*

*For my good friend, David Gish, whose engineer's cap I wear with pride.*

*For James Jenkins, who believed in the book sight unseen.*

*For Dr. Norman Field who is generous and good.*

*For Tracey Nation, Sharon and Melissa Mudd for their generous input.*

*For Douglas Blaine and Bachmann Trains for help and kindness.*

*For the Formosa Chinese Café', who kindly tolerated our meetings.*

*For my publisher, James Wright, who gently and patiently engineered this whole process and who has my eternal gratitude.*

*And most importantly, thank you Lord for the strength and courage to persevere.*

# Chapter One

# Tinker Time

Once upon a very special time, way up in the ice-white land of the North Pole, there lived a group of elves. The elves' work was to assist Santa with all the happenings for Christmas. Only extraordinary elves, who possess much love and dedication, can spend their lives in the service of Santa Claus. Tinker was just such an elf.

From the beginning, Tinker had dreamed of becoming one of Santa's chosen. All through school, he had thought of little else. He had not played baseball or soccer or even ice hockey. Instead, Tinker had devoted his time to preparing himself to being the best elf he could be, with the hope that one day he would become a Christmas Elf. Tinker took classes in arts and crafts, design and carpentry. He rebuilt engines, studied electronics, and computer science. He joined the chorus and the band, learned to bake and even how to sew. When the invitation came to become one of Santa's helpers, Tinker was ready. He was prepared in every way — every way except *one.*

Tinker suffered from acute clumsiness. Always anxious to please, the poor boy blundered from one mishap to another. He was viewed by the other elves as an accident in motion. Tinker constantly bumped, bumbled, tumbled, crashed, or careened into something or someone. Some of the elves avoided Tinker—not because they did not like him, but for their own safety. Accidents just somehow seemed to happen whenever Tinker was around.

Everyone knew of Tinker's "exception," even Santa, but it did not matter to

Santa. He rather considered it an opportunity to develop exceptional talent. As soon as Tinker arrived at Christmas Village, Santa immediately saw the goodness in the young elf's heart. But as soon as Tinker saw Santa, he immediately tripped and collided into a group of elves. Like a row of dominoes, all the elves fell one after another. Tinker quickly scrambled up from the ground and offered a hand to each elf as he apologized. As Tinker helped the last fallen elf to his feet, the young fellow remarked, "Glad you could *drop* by." Tinker's face flushed pink as the other elves snickered.

Santa looked on in silence. His heart hurt for Tinker, and both he and Mrs. Claus fretted over Tinker's exception. Each tried to think of some way in which

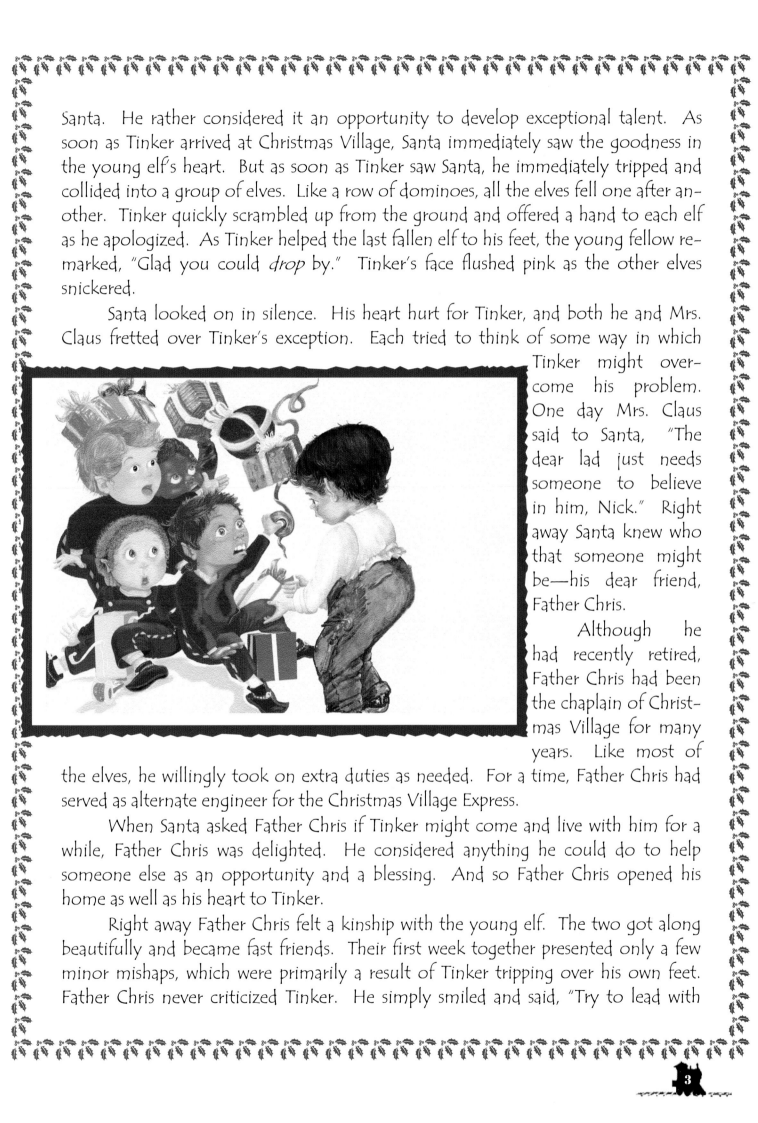

Tinker might overcome his problem. One day Mrs. Claus said to Santa, "The dear lad just needs someone to believe in him, Nick." Right away Santa knew who that someone might be—his dear friend, Father Chris.

Although he had recently retired, Father Chris had been the chaplain of Christmas Village for many years. Like most of the elves, he willingly took on extra duties as needed. For a time, Father Chris had served as alternate engineer for the Christmas Village Express.

When Santa asked Father Chris if Tinker might come and live with him for a while, Father Chris was delighted. He considered anything he could do to help someone else as an opportunity and a blessing. And so Father Chris opened his home as well as his heart to Tinker.

Right away Father Chris felt a kinship with the young elf. The two got along beautifully and became fast friends. Their first week together presented only a few minor mishaps, which were primarily a result of Tinker tripping over his own feet. Father Chris never criticized Tinker. He simply smiled and said, "Try to lead with your heart, Tinker. Trust it. It will not fail you even when you fall."

Tinker soon recognized that, like Santa, Father Chris was always good and kind. It was not in the old elf's nature to be anything else. And like Santa, Father Chris soon saw the goodness in Tinker's heart. Both Santa and Father Chris believed that

Tinker's clumsiness was a result of his lack of confidence, and both made extra efforts to help the young elf believe in himself.

Since Santa had asked Father Chris to determine where Tinker's talents would be most helpful, Father Chris created various projects for the two of them. They made toys, cooked candy, baked goodies, printed cards, bound books, and generally tried making most everything. Under Father Chris's gentle tutoring, Tinker worked well, but Father Chris was most impressed with Tinker's ability to work with animals. Tinker seemed to relax and be himself around them. Animals can read a person's heart, and when they read Tinker's, they read the love and respect that was there for them.

Father Chris enjoyed Tinker's company, and as far as he was concerned, Tinker could have stayed on at his cottage indefinitely. But about three months into his stay, an accident occurred. While Tinker was emptying the ashes in the fireplace, he unknowingly bumped the damper, causing it to close. Later when Tinker decided to surprise Father Chris with some roasted marshmallows, smoke instantly filled the room. Within moments, the air inside the cottage was thick and hazy with the gray vapor. A neighbor observed smoke billowing from the cottage and telephoned the Fire Department.

With bells ringing and sirens sounding, the Fire Department arrived with all the clamor, noise, and excitement a fire alarm brings. The firemen soon discovered that the closed damper was the source of the problem.

As the firemen worked, Tinker stood outside looking rather heartsick and sad. At his side, he still held the stick topped with the unmelted marshmallows. Chuckling among themselves, some of the firemen shook their heads in amazement.. "Boy," one of them said, "you're the only person I've ever seen that's dangerous with a marshmallow." With that, the other firemen laughed. Tinker's cheeks flushed a crimson red.

As a practical joke, the firemen issued a warning:

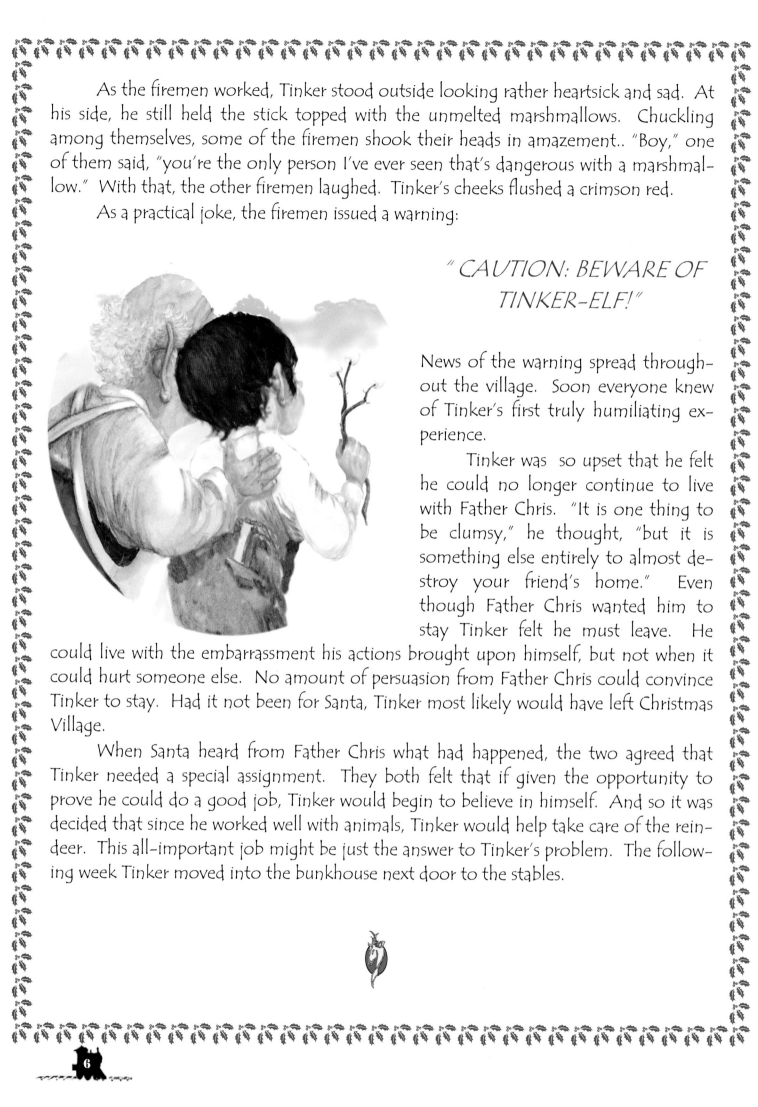

## "CAUTION: BEWARE OF TINKER-ELF!"

News of the warning spread throughout the village. Soon everyone knew of Tinker's first truly humiliating experience.

Tinker was so upset that he felt he could no longer continue to live with Father Chris. "It is one thing to be clumsy," he thought, "but it is something else entirely to almost destroy your friend's home." Even though Father Chris wanted him to stay Tinker felt he must leave. He could live with the embarrassment his actions brought upon himself, but not when it could hurt someone else. No amount of persuasion from Father Chris could convince Tinker to stay. Had it not been for Santa, Tinker most likely would have left Christmas Village.

When Santa heard from Father Chris what had happened, the two agreed that Tinker needed a special assignment. They both felt that if given the opportunity to prove he could do a good job, Tinker would begin to believe in himself. And so it was decided that since he worked well with animals, Tinker would help take care of the reindeer. This all-important job might be just the answer to Tinker's problem. The following week Tinker moved into the bunkhouse next door to the stables.

# Chapter Two

# Reindeer Rally

Tinker was thrilled with his first official assignment. He put his heart and soul into taking good care of the reindeer. He brushed their fur coats each and every day. And no matter what the weather, Tinker saw that the reindeer were always exercised. They had to stay in good condition for their yearly run around the world.

Tinker enjoyed feeding the reindeer, talking to each one in turn as he passed out their food. With Tinker in charge, the reindeer were fed regularly and always on time, and usually with only minor mishaps. But one night Tinker tripped and accidentally dumped a bucket of mash right on top of Comet's head. Comet, who was napping at the time, was so startled to awaken to a mushy bucket of mash on her head that she bolted out of the barn like a rocket. Limber and fast, Comet streaked across Christmas Courtyard before Tinker could barely blink.

At the same time that Comet was racing across the Courtyard, Santa was taking a leisurely stroll. Suddenly, Comet came crashing through the bushes. On sight of

Santa, Comet attempted to stop. Quickly, she dug her hooves into the ice, but instead of stopping, her sudden slow-down simply caused her to slide hurry-scurry across the ice. Frightened and confused, Comet landed in a crumpled heap at Santa's feet.

Santa studied the forlorn face of the reindeer in front of him. Slowly, he knelt

beside her and gently wiped away the remaining morsels of mash. Stroking her sleek and slender body, Santa calmed the frightened reindeer. Comet nuzzled Santa's hand, and Santa stayed at her side until Tinker could catch up with them. By the next day, everyone in Christmas Village was aware of what had happened, even though Santa had said nothing to anyone. Secretly, Tinker was referred to as "reindeer rocket fuel." The incident was yet another source of shame and embarrassment for him.

Unfortunately, the mishap with Comet was not Tinker's greatest reindeer blunder. On the last Christmas Eve that Tinker tended the reindeer, he had been instructed to have Santa's sleigh hitched by four p.m. for the all-important Christmas Eve run. When Santa came out to board the sleigh, it was fully packed and ready to go. Mrs. Claus and all the elves were gathered to bid Santa farewell. Everything and everyone was ready and accounted for except for the nine reindeer and Tinker, and there was no sign of them.

Whispering among themselves, all the elves meandered about the sleigh bewildered by the missing reindeer.

Uriah, the Head-of-Operations elf, had been checking over last minute details. When he caught sight of the unhitched sleigh with no reindeer to be seen, he shouted, "Oh, my word! Who's in charge here?" Suddenly he remembered, "Tinker! I should have known!"

Just at that moment, Tinker appeared with the reindeer. He was not exactly leading the reindeer. Actually, they were kind of leading him. All the reins were wadded together, and Tinker was dead center in the middle of the reindeer, trying desperately to hang on to the wad of reins. He looked for all the world like a miniature maypole with nine reindeer around him.

What had taken so long was that the group—Tinker, reindeer, and wad of reins—had to move in unison or they did not move at all. The precision of it was truly quite remarkable. And it was only through the efforts of Tinker's calm coaxing that they were even able to move. At anytime other than the last minute on Christmas Eve, the sight of Tinker tied up with nine reindeer might have been amusing. But at this time of year in Christmas Village, an act such as this would be considered somewhere close to treason.

With fiery eyes like those of a raging dragon, Uriah glared at Tinker. At that moment, Uriah's angry eyes looked as though they might turn Tinker to stone.

Tinker took in a deep breath and uttered a quick prayer that he would not be banished from Christmas Village.

With considerable maneuvering, it took several elves more than ten minutes, giggling as they went, to get Tinker undone from the reindeer and the reindeer undone from each other. Tinker kept his head down and would have cried had it not been for further humiliating himself. He knew that as soon as Santa was not around, the other elves would laugh and make fun of him.

After the reindeer were untangled and hitched to the sleigh, Santa went around to each one, patting its head and calling it by name. There was something special in Santa's voice that soothed the spirit and calmed the senses, and here it reassured the reindeer.

As Santa adjusted himself into the seat of the sleigh, he took a moment to study the sight of the forlorn Tinker, who stood as solemn as a sentry, while the other elves shuffled about trying to muffle their laughter. All of a sudden Santa called out, "Tinker, my friend, how would you like to come with me on this trip? " I promise you, it's a journey you'll not soon forget. And I could use the help."

Uriah opened his mouth to protest, but Santa shook his head, indicating to Uriah not to say anything. All the elves stopped and stared, their eyes and mouths open wide in amazement. No one had ever accompanied Santa before!

Tinker's eyes and mouth were probably opened the widest, for no one was more amazed than he. He stuttered three times before he could even answer. "Uh, uh, uh, yes, yes, sir. I'd be proud, sir! And I promise not to touch anything!"

"Well, I was kind of hoping you would help me. And I'm afraid you won't be much help if that's the case," Santa teased. "Climb aboard, Tinker. I think we'll do just fine."

Uriah just shook his head in frustration, and the other elves remained frozen in shock.

As Santa, Tinker, and the reindeer pulled away, Tinker's heart swelled with love for this kindliest of elves. Like all the elves, Tinker loved Santa. He wished he could be like Santa.

As they flew across the early afternoon sky, Santa said, "Tinker, it's good to have you aboard."

"Thank you, sir," Tinker whispered. He wanted to say more, but the words would not come.

Santa sensed this, and when silence alone filled the air, he added, "We must all try not to let situations get the best of us, Tinker, because the best of us belongs elsewhere."

"Yes, sir," Tinker said.

"We all have a gift, and gifts are to be shared. The more a gift is shared, the better it becomes," Santa explained.

Tinker smiled and nodded in agreement.

"Life has a way of leading us to where we're supposed to be," Santa continued, "and it's what we learn along the way that makes the difference. It's the journey that's important, Tinker, not the vehicle, not the time of arrival, but what we arrive with, what we learn throughout our journey. Do you understand what I am saying to you, son?" Santa asked.

"Yes, sir. I think so, sir," Tinker answered. "But what is my gift? What could I possibly have to offer?"

Santa turned to look directly at Tinker. "You have yourself, Tinker. That is your gift. And just like building a barn, sometimes a gift takes time to put together. And often times, the more difficult the task, the greater the gift. Your gift is there. You must simply allow it to surface."

"I so want to believe that, Santa," Tinker replied.

With a gleam in his eyes, Santa leaned over and whispered,

*"Then do.
That's all it
Takes."*

The two sat in silence for a long time as Tinker thought about what Santa had said. Then suddenly Santa asked, "Want to try your hand with these reins, Tinker?"

Tinker turned pale, and his dark eyes looked like two little pieces of coal against the pallor of his face. "Oh, no, sir! Not a chance! It would be disaster for sure!"

"Believe, Tinker. *You must believe.*" Santa repeated.

Throughout the trip, Tinker studied the reins. More than anything, he wanted to take hold of them, but past memories would not let him.

Santa sensed the struggle that was going on inside Tinker. Patting the young elf on the back, he said, "In time, Tinker, in time."

Like tracks in new-fallen snow, life often leads us to where we're supposed to be. The job of taking care of the reindeer was just one path Tinker would take along the way to becoming who he was meant to be.

# Chapter Three

# Tinker's Toys

After the catastrophe with the tangled reindeer, Uriah decided it was best for all to assign Tinker to another job. With all the newfangled, electrical toys and gizmos, the elves working in production were finding it increasingly difficult to keep up with demand. With some hesitation, Uriah decided to assign Tinker to work as a mechanic's assistant in toy production. Although Uriah found the thought of Tinker working with mechanical and electrical toys frightening, his needs outweighed his fears. "Please, try not to blow up the place, Tinker," Uriah scolded as he issued the assignment.

To everyone's surprise, Tinker, who at times seemed to have difficulty simply walking, was exceptionally good with electrical and mechanical toys. By mid-day of his first day on the job, Tinker had met his daily quota of finished toys. And to the amazement of the other elves, Tinker's toys worked beautifully. They ran smoothly, did not break, and all parts were soundly secured. As a matter of fact, Tinker's toys ran more smoothly than those of some of the older, more experienced elves. This surprised no one more than Tinker.

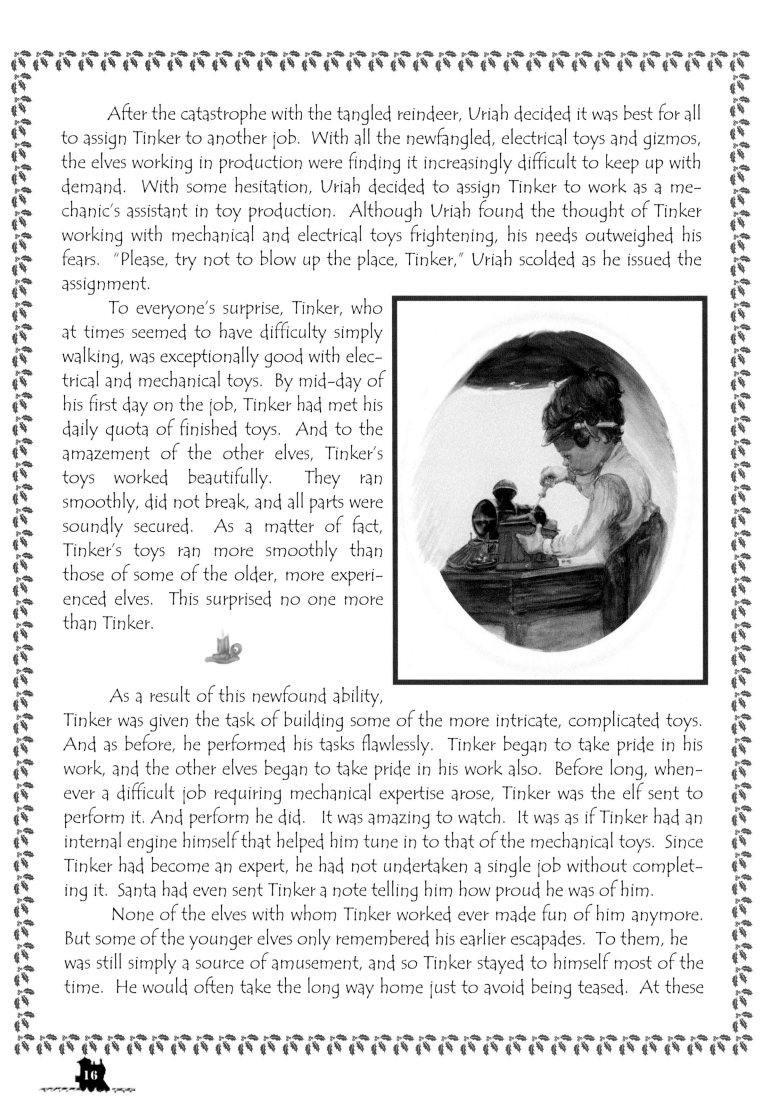

As a result of this newfound ability, Tinker was given the task of building some of the more intricate, complicated toys. And as before, he performed his tasks flawlessly. Tinker began to take pride in his work, and the other elves began to take pride in his work also. Before long, whenever a difficult job requiring mechanical expertise arose, Tinker was the elf sent to perform it. And perform he did. It was amazing to watch. It was as if Tinker had an internal engine himself that helped him tune in to that of the mechanical toys. Since Tinker had become an expert, he had not undertaken a single job without completing it. Santa had even sent Tinker a note telling him how proud he was of him.

None of the elves with whom Tinker worked ever made fun of him anymore. But some of the younger elves only remembered his earlier escapades. To them, he was still simply a source of amusement, and so Tinker stayed to himself most of the time. He would often take the long way home just to avoid being teased. At these times, it seemed that the more Tinker was taunted, the clumsier he became. He began spending more and more time alone, and sometimes the loneliness was difficult to bear. He missed the good times he had shared with Father Chris.

And Father Chris missed Tinker. When retirement came, Father Chris found he did not like it very much. He had worked for so long that he didn't know how to retire, and although Father Chris tried to keep busy, retirement was like someone else's glove that just didn't fit. And after Tinker moved out, Father Chris felt lonely for the first time.

As happenstance would have it, at this very same time, Rudy, the Chief Engineer, was suddenly called home to help out on his family's Christmas tree farm. As Father Chris had once been an alternate engineer, he was called in to help.

Father Chris had always understood the importance of playing on a team. With Father Chris at the controls, he and the old steam engine would be as certain as sunrise. The rather ram-shackled, old engine was a lot like Father Chris—showing age but still work-worthy.

Besides her tinder, Engine No. 25 pulled three passenger cars and a dining car around the shops and stores of Christmas Village. The old steam engine carried the hardworking elves back and forth from their homes to work and then home again.

According to Engineer Rudy, the old engine's first puff of steam sounded a lot like a sneeze, so he nicknamed her "Ah-Choo." Whenever her first burst of steam would billow forth each day, Rudy would yell, "God bless you!" Soon everyone in Christmas Village began referring to the old engine as "Ah-Choo," and some would even say "God bless you" as she chugged past.

Because of Tinker's success as a mechanic in the Toy Department, he was assigned the position of Chief Mechanic for the Village Express.

Late on a Friday night, Father Chris engineered steam engine "Ah-Choo" to the roundhouse for her yearly check-up. There she would be poked, probed, and prodded until all kinks, clinks, and catches were clearly gone. Tinker had been alerted and was waiting for them. Father Chris could see Tinker in the distance, waving a bright yellow lantern to motion him and Engine No. 25 into the problem stall at the roundhouse.

Tinker leaned forward with his head slightly cocked to one side as he listened to the steam engine. "She seems to be running a bit sluggish," he said.

"This cold and this late at night, wouldn't you be a bit sluggish, too?" Father Chris teased as he stepped down from the train.

"You got that right," Tinker agreed as he greeted his friend with a hug. As he studied the old engine, Tinker said, "Well, let's take a listen to her."

While Tinker examined "Ah-Choo," Father Chris stood nearby. After a while, Tinker asked Father Chris to kindle the old engine's fire with more coal. Tinker watched closely as fire from the burning coal heated the water in the boiler. As Father Chris gently pulled the throttle to release steam, Tinker began to circle "Ah-Choo," climbing over, under, and across her. As a doctor listens intently to a patient's heart, Tinker listened to the movement of steam as injectors moved steam through the engine. Before long, Tinker had solved the problem. A piece of metal had slipped out of place in the old train's chimney, blocking the passage of some of the hot steam that moved "Ah-Choo" along. Tinker secured the metal piece into place and greased and lubricated each and every joint of the old train. In no time, "Ah-Choo" was once again running as smoothly as reindeer across a Christmas Eve sky. Come Monday morning, old "Ah-Choo" would strut her steam around the Village track—all sound and secure. Tinker was pleased.

Father Chris shook his head in disbelief, "Son, you are a wonder!"

Tinker blushed. "Only because you and Santa believed in me. I was ready to give up and go home. I'll always be grateful."

"In that case," Father Chris said, "maybe you won't mind doing a little favor for me?"

"Of course, anything. What is it you need?" Tinker asked.

"I'd like for you to come out to the cottage on Sunday and have lunch with me. I miss your company," Father Chris said.

"And I yours," Tinker replied. "I'd love to come for a visit."

"Oh, and by the way," Father Chris added, "My niece, Pixie, will be there. She arrived yesterday, and she'll be staying with me for a while. I thought maybe you could help me entertain her."

Tinker paled instantly, as he was very shy, especially around girls. He tried to protest, but he was so stunned that no sound passed his lips.

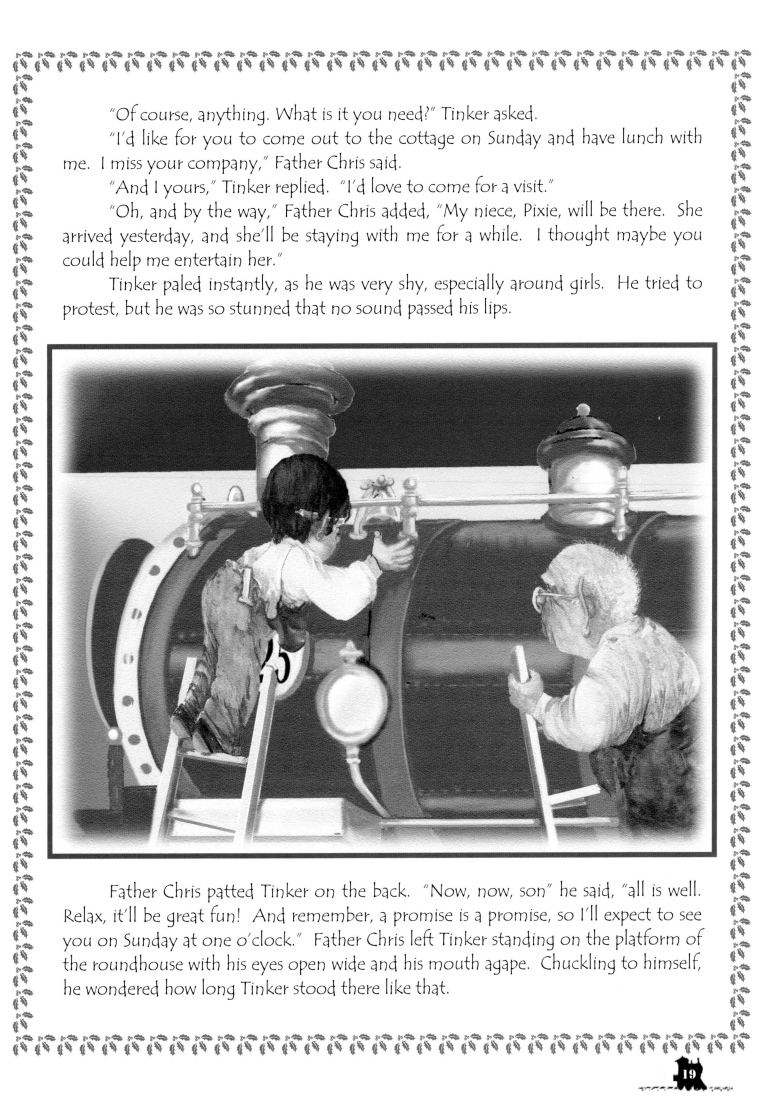

Father Chris patted Tinker on the back. "Now, now, son" he said, "all is well. Relax, it'll be great fun! And remember, a promise is a promise, so I'll expect to see you on Sunday at one o'clock." Father Chris left Tinker standing on the platform of the roundhouse with his eyes open wide and his mouth agape. Chuckling to himself, he wondered how long Tinker stood there like that.

As for Tinker, he appeared to be in a trance for the rest of the week. All his thoughts funneled into one—–

*"A girl! How do I act around a girl?"*

# Chapter Four

## Light Up My Life

The following Sunday, Tinker appeared at the door to Father Chris's cottage as promised. He stood there for nearly ten minutes before he could bring himself to knock. Actually he never did knock, even though he tried. When he would lift his hand, it would just hang in mid-air like it was frozen. And although his hand never touched the door, the door suddenly opened.

"Tinker, my boy, there you are! I was beginning to worry about you," Father Chris said.

"Please come inside and warm yourself. You look positively frozen."

Tinker *was* frozen—frozen from fear. When he did not move, Father Chris stepped beside Tinker and gently nudged him inside. "Like I said," Father Chris added as he pushed Tinker ever so slightly forward, "frozen, positively frozen. Pixie, dear, how about a cup of hot chocolate for our guest?"

Tinker's eyes followed the direction of Father Chris's gaze. If he were indeed frozen, he surely melted when he saw the petite vision of loveliness passing before him. A beautiful, young girl moved across the room as gracefully as a willow in the wind. Tinker wondered if he would ever be able to breathe again.

With Father Chris nudging him forward, Tinker eventually reached the hearth of the open fire. Since Tinker's eyes never left Pixie's direction, helping Tinker remove his outerwear took considerable effort on Father Chris's part. Tinker was of no help, as he appeared to be hypnotized. And when Father Chris tried to remove Tinker's leggings, Tinker slipped and almost fell into the fireplace.

When Pixie returned, a brightly blushing Tinker was sprawled across the floor in front of the fireplace with his leggings hanging half-off his feet. "Oh, my! Are you all right?" she asked.

Tinker's face glowed like Rudolph's nose. If he could have melted like snow and seeped through the floor, he would have.

Father Chris quickly spoke up on Tinker's behalf. "Oh, dear, I'm afraid I hindered you, Tinker, when what I was trying to do was help. I'm so very sorry, my friend. I did not mean to make you fall."

"Oh, no," Tinker replied, "it was my fault entirely." Shyly, Tinker glanced towards Pixie and then back to Father Chris. "Guess I forgot to lift my leg."

Father Chris suddenly began sniffing the air. "Do you smell something burning? Pixie, dear, did you remember to turn the kettle off?"

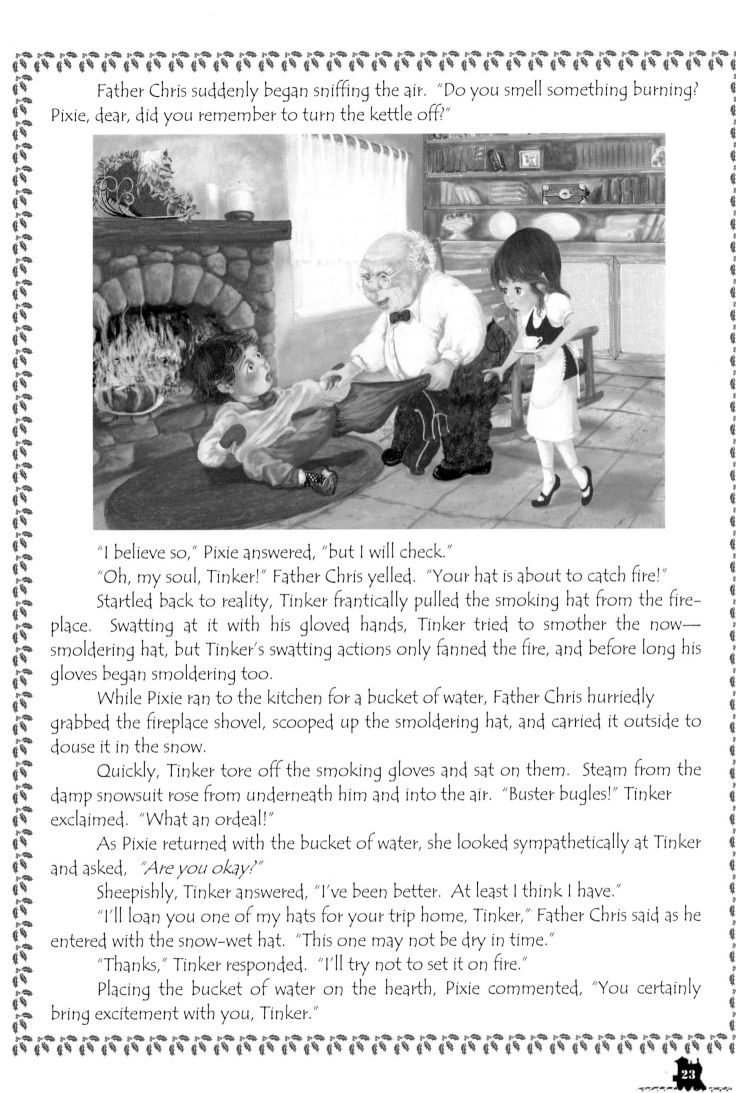

"I believe so," Pixie answered, "but I will check."

"Oh, my soul, Tinker!" Father Chris yelled. "Your hat is about to catch fire!"

Startled back to reality, Tinker frantically pulled the smoking hat from the fireplace. Swatting at it with his gloved hands, Tinker tried to smother the now—smoldering hat, but Tinker's swatting actions only fanned the fire, and before long his gloves began smoldering too.

While Pixie ran to the kitchen for a bucket of water, Father Chris hurriedly grabbed the fireplace shovel, scooped up the smoldering hat, and carried it outside to douse it in the snow.

Quickly, Tinker tore off the smoking gloves and sat on them. Steam from the damp snowsuit rose from underneath him and into the air. "Buster bugles!" Tinker exclaimed. "What an ordeal!"

As Pixie returned with the bucket of water, she looked sympathetically at Tinker and asked, *"Are you okay?"*

Sheepishly, Tinker answered, "I've been better. At least I think I have."

"I'll loan you one of my hats for your trip home, Tinker," Father Chris said as he entered with the snow-wet hat. "This one may not be dry in time."

"Thanks," Tinker responded. "I'll try not to set it on fire."

Placing the bucket of water on the hearth, Pixie commented, "You certainly bring excitement with you, Tinker."

"It seems to follow me wherever I go," Tinker replied as he rose from the floor. "Personally, I could do without it, or at least a little less of it."

"Oh, but no!" Pixie said as she flashed Tinker her most unguarded smile. "It makes it all so much more fun. I'm afraid not much ever happens to me, and I fear I must be very boring."

"Pixie is an only child, Tinker," Father Chris explained. "And I'm afraid we've all been guilty of trying to protect her. As a matter of fact, she has been reminding me that she is never going to learn anything about life if she's never allowed to experience it."

Pixie rolled her dark brown eyes at her uncle and smiled. "Yes, but love should allow for growth as well as protection. Don't you think so. Tinker?"

Tinker looked first at Father Chris and then at Pixie. "Well, uh, I guess that uh," Tinker suddenly stopped. "I sure am hungry, and I know I smell something besides a toasted hat."

Father Chris and Pixie both laughed. Taking Tinker by the arm and leading him into the kitchen, Father Chris responded, "And you're also quite the diplomat, Tinker, and very smooth. You slid out of that with all the grace of a greased gummy worm."

All three laughed and shared pleasant banter back and forth as they sat down to a sumptuous Sunday lunch. In addition to all the excitement the day had already brought, events were about to unfold that would change Tinker's life forever.

# Chapter Five

# A Sudden Surprise

As Father Chris, Pixie, and Tinker talked after lunch, there was a knock at the door. To their surprise, it was Santa. He looked tired, and something was obviously weighing on his mind. Tinker offered Santa his seat by the fire, and Pixie brought Santa a cup of hot chocolate.

No one said anything for what seemed like a long time as Santa studied the steam rising from the cup of hot chocolate.

Father Chris finally asked, "Nick, what's on your mind?"

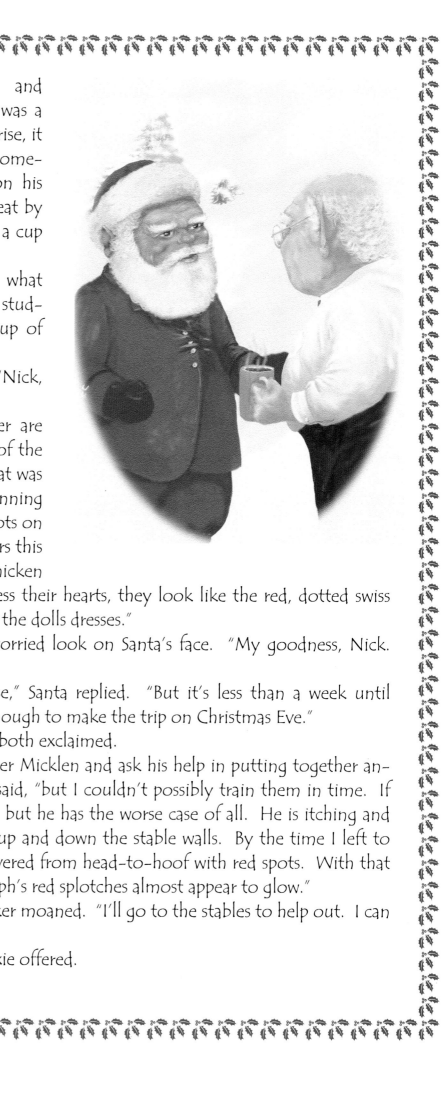

Santa sighed, "The reindeer are sick. I've been with them most of the night. At first, I didn't know what was wrong. They were listless and running a fever, and then I noticed red spots on them. The vet confirmed my fears this morning. The reindeer have chicken pox, every last one of them. Bless their hearts, they look like the red, dotted swiss fabric we sometimes use to make the dolls dresses."

Father Chris studied the worried look on Santa's face. "My goodness, Nick. What can we do?"

"They'll be okay, of course," Santa replied. "But it's less than a week until Christmas. They won't be well enough to make the trip on Christmas Eve."

"Oh, no!" Tinker and Pixie both exclaimed.

"I could go to Forest Ranger Micklen and ask his help in putting together another team for this year," Santa said, "but I couldn't possibly train them in time. If only Rudolph could guide them, but he has the worse case of all. He is itching and scratching and rubbing his sides up and down the stable walls. By the time I left to come here, he was absolutely covered from head-to-hoof with red spots. With that beautiful nose of his, poor Rudolph's red splotches almost appear to glow."

"Oh, the poor things," Tinker moaned. "I'll go to the stables to help out. I can give them some oatmeal baths."

"I could help with that," Pixie offered.

"That's a good idea," Father Chris said. Turning to Santa, he added, "We can all help, Nick. What else can we do?"

Again, Santa did not respond for what seemed like a long time. Looking intensely at Father Chris, he said, "I would like to use the train."

The wide-eyed look on Father Chris's face captured his surprise. "What!" he gasped.

Tinker was so amazed that his voice squeaked, "In the sky? You want to put the train in the sky?"

Pixie softly chimed, "Oh, my!"

Father Chris and Santa stared into one another's eyes.

As the surprise of Santa's suggestion settled across their faces, Tinker ventured a response. "I think it would work," he said. "I'd have to make some modifications, but I think we could make it work."

"How quickly could you make it work?" Santa asked as he studied Tinker's face. "Could you make it work within a week?"

"Oh, Nick, that's a big request!" Father Chris remarked. "You and I both know Tinker has the talent and ability, but he would have to have time to make it happen."

Quickly, Tinker looked from one to the other. "I can make it work within a day. I just don't know about landing on rooftops."

"Oh, my," Father Chris sighed. "I hadn't thought of that."

After a moment's consideration, Santa said, "Well, it would help if we could land on rooftops, but if you can't make it happen, we'll just have to adjust."

"But, Nick, you can't possibly add an additional step to the procedure," Father Chris pointed out. "You'd be exhausted before you got a hundred miles from home."

"What else are we to do, Chris?" Santa asked. "We could take along some extra help. Not much, mind you, otherwise we'll be tripping all over ourselves."

"I could help," Pixie suggested.

Just as Father Chris was about to respond to Pixie's offer, Tinker interrupted, "If we unhitched the other cars and only used the engine and tinder, I think we could do it. I think we *could* land on rooftops. We'll have to modify the wheels somewhat, but that shouldn't be a problem."

"Tinker, son, I know you truly want to help," Father Chris sighed again. "But I

have never tried to engineer a train across the sky, not to mention land it on a roof."

"Well, what we need is a place to practice," Tinker suggested.

Santa thought for a moment, then said, "There's that old deserted farm just south of town. As I recall, it has a barn and a tool shed in addition to the farmhouse. I'd have to check, but we could probably practice there."

"Great!" Tinker exclaimed. "Let's do it!"

Father Chris lowered his head somewhat as he solemnly said, "I have another problem." Everyone turned their attention in his direction. "I have a dreadful fear of heights. Climbing aboard a train is about as high as I ever venture to climb."

Santa rubbed his chin thoughtfully. "I see," he said. "That does present a problem."

"I'm sorry," Father Chris added.

Before Santa could respond, Tinker quickly offered. "I could do it! I could engineer the train! I'd need some help with shoveling the coal, but Mathias could help me there. And he doesn't take up much room."

Santa and Father Chris looked first at one another and then quizzically at Tinker. At the very same time, they both inquired. "Mathias?"

"Oh," Tinker replied hesitantly, "he's my roommate, kind of."

Santa and Father Chris exchanged looks of surprise.

"He's a friend?" Santa asked. "Why haven't I heard of him before?"

"Well, sir," Tinker answered, "I've sort of kept him a secret."

"But why?" Father Chris asked.

Cautiously, Tinker continued, "He's a, he's a monkey, sir."

Pixie's eyes grew large with delight as she stifled a giggle.

Again, Santa and Father Chris exchanged looks of surprise.

"A monkey?" Father Chris inquired.

Tinker stuttered, "Well, actually, he's uh, he's a chimp—a chimpanzee to be exact. My uncle, who used to work in the circus, brought him to me when he came to visit recently."

"Oh, how exciting!" Pixie squealed.

"Tinker, it's wonderful that you obviously have a talented friend," Father Chris responded. "But I don't think you can count on a monkey to help you with something like this. It's going to be a difficult job at best. You would have to have one of

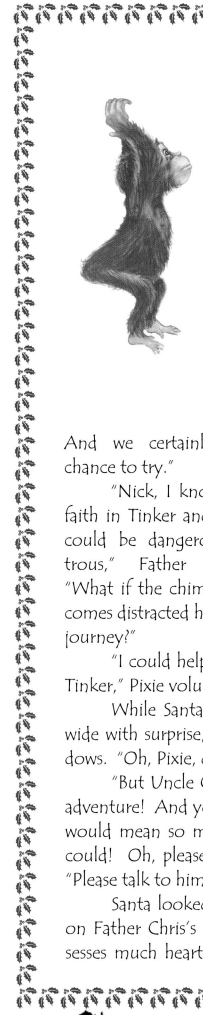

the other elves help you."

Blinking back the tears that filled his eyes, Tinker replied, "Can you think of one other elf who would be willing to help me with something like this?" Tinker's chin quivered ever so slightly as he looked away.

Pixie reached across and gently placed her hand on Tinker's shoulder. Warmed by Pixie's kind gesture, Tinker half-smiled.

"If Tinker says he and the chimp can do it, then I think they can," Santa firmly stated. "Tinker has never let me down.

And we certainly owe him the chance to try."

"Nick, I know you have great faith in Tinker and so do I, but this could be dangerous, if not disastrous," Father Chris remarked. "What if the chimp tires out or becomes distracted halfway through the journey?"

"I could help! I would go with Tinker," Pixie volunteered.

While Santa smiled at the sincerity of Pixie's offer, Father Chris's eyes grew wide with surprise, and his face turned the color of the frost that covered the windows. "Oh, Pixie, dear, I don't think so," he mumbled.

"But Uncle Chris, I could help, I know I could! It would be such a wonderful adventure! And you said yourself that I've always been sheltered from everything. It would mean so much to me—to be able to help, and I could do this. I know I could! Oh, please, Uncle Chris, don't say no." Pixie turned to Santa and pleaded, "Please talk to him, Santa. Help him understand!"

Santa looked lovingly at the young elf then walked over and placed his hand on Father Chris's shoulder. "She's young, Chris, but, like you, she obviously possesses much heart. And I can surely appreciate your concern, but we would take good care of her. You know that." Santa paused for a moment before continuing. "The task before us is going to require exceptional talent and dedication, and Pixie has that, as does Tinker. With their help and with yours, we can make this happen."

As Father Chris considered what Santa had said, he sighed a deep, heavy sigh that shook his whole body. "I don't have to tell you that this is hard," he replied. "You lead with your heart, Nick. You always have. And that's why we follow." The old elf thought for a moment more. "But you're right—Pixie is exceptional! And I know that the time is nigh for Pixie to become the person she's meant to be. I cannot say I am not concerned. And yet how can I refuse? As hard as it is to let go, there is no one to whom I'd rather entrust her than you, Nick."

Father Chris stood, and with a heavy heart he turned to Pixie. With her small face in his hands, he said, "Go with care, child. Go with grace. Go with God, and know that you are loved."

Pixie hugged her beloved uncle.

"Is anything more beautiful than the love of a child?" Santa asked. "Thank you, Chris. We will regard her as precious cargo. Isn't that right, Tinker?"

"Oh, yes, of course," Tinker quickly replied. "I would never do anything to endanger Pixie."

Father Chris looked first at Santa and then at Tinker. "That goes without saying. But sometimes things happen over which we have no control. It's those times that concern me."

"And as you well know," Santa said, "it's during those times we simply must rely on our faith to guide us. When we believe, miracles happen, and after all, belief is what we're all about." Santa paused then added, "Of course, as always we must proceed with caution. And certain things I think we should keep quiet for now. I am specifically referring to the chimp, Tinker."

"Understood," Tinker answered.

"Oh, I can't wait!" Pixie declared. "What do we do first? How can I help? When do we get started?"

Santa and Tinker laughed as Father Chris placed his arm around Pixie's shoulder. "Would you guess she's a little excited?" he said.

"When can you have the modifications to the train completed?" Santa asked Tinker.

"Tomorrow, possibly by the end of the day, sir," Tinker responded.

"Good," said Santa. "We'll practice the following day. I'll check and see if we can use the old farm south of here." As Santa sauntered to the door, Father Chris followed. "Please try not to worry, Chris," he said. "Everything is going to be fine. We treasure Pixie and will take good care of her, won't we, Tinker?"

"Yes, sir," Tinker quickly answered. "Good care! The very best care! You have my word." Tinker smiled at Pixie, who blushed and smiled.

"And it would probably be a good idea for Pixie and the chimp to spend some time together," Santa suggested. "Tinker could go over the procedure as to what will be expected, and Pixie can begin training the chimp. Practice always makes us more efficient."

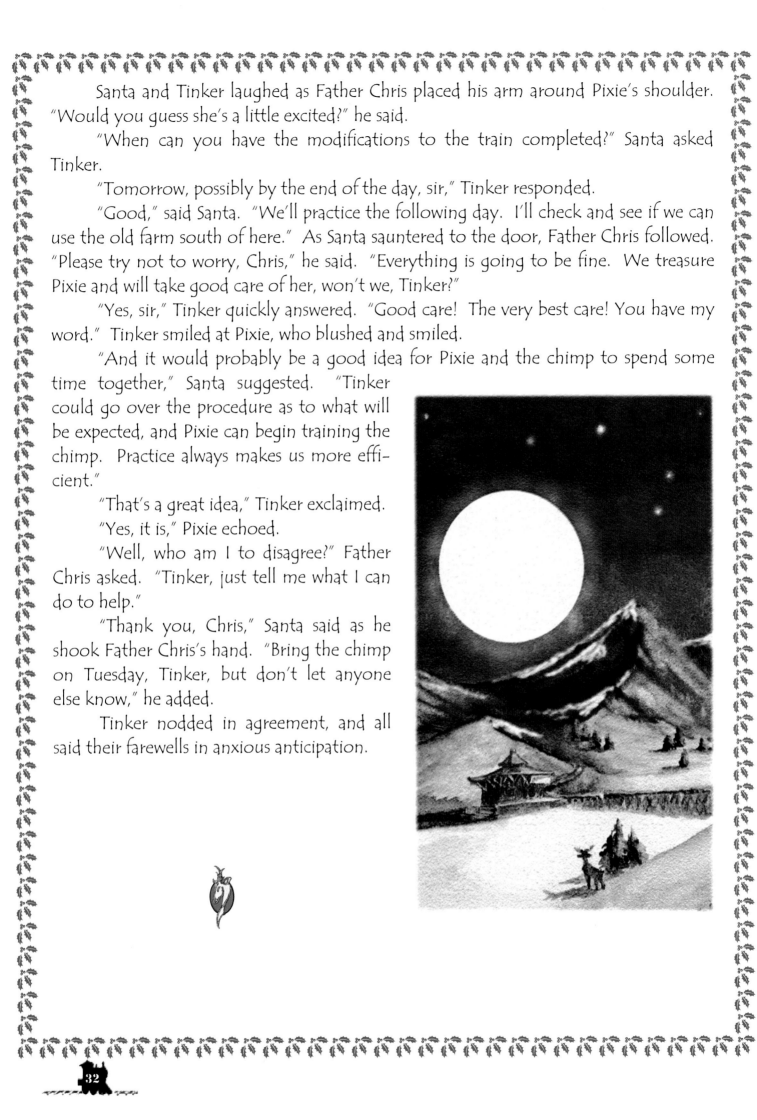

"That's a great idea," Tinker exclaimed.

"Yes, it is," Pixie echoed.

"Well, who am I to disagree?" Father Chris asked. "Tinker, just tell me what I can do to help."

"Thank you, Chris," Santa said as he shook Father Chris's hand. "Bring the chimp on Tuesday, Tinker, but don't let anyone else know," he added.

Tinker nodded in agreement, and all said their farewells in anxious anticipation.

# Chapter Six

# Engine, Engine No. 25

Tinker's excitement was so great he felt that he was going to burst. He hardly slept at all that night. At first sight of dawn, he was eagerly up and happily at work. His first task was to design a steel runner to be attached underneath the wheels. The runner would be similar to skis but with a higher, more circular curve at the front. About mid-morning, Tinker stopped work on the modification to take Mathias to Pixie. Like Tinker, Mathias immediately warmed to Pixie, and the little chimp barely even noticed when Tinker left.

By the time Father Chris arrived at the roundhouse, Tinker had completed the design for the runner. As Tinker continued working, Father Chris took the design to the steel shop. Tinker kept a running list of parts or tools that he needed, and Father Chris would fetch them for him.

While Father Chris was gone to pick up a special lamp to be attached to the front of the engine, Santa arrived to see how things were going. For a few moments, Santa quietly observed Tinker, who was completely absorbed in his work. Santa's heart was warmed by Tinker's obvious commitment. "Well, you certainly seem to have everything under control." he said. "Thought I might be of some help, but I believe I would just be in your way."

With a pencil stuck behind each ear, Tinker looked up from his drawing table. "You could never be in the way," he said. "I want to show you something." Tinker picked up a box with wires hanging out of it. "It's a navigational device that I'm going to attach to the engine to help us track where we are." Then, almost apologetically, he added, "I know you don't need it, sir, but it will help me."

Santa studied the box for a minute, then looked at Tinker. "That's fine, son. Whatever helps." Then with a mischievous grin, Santa said, "But I suspect you know where you are now."

As a broad grin of sudden awareness seemed to burst across his face, Tinker said, "You intend for me to take the controls, don't you, sir? Whether it's the reins of the sleigh or the controls of the train?"

With that magnificent twinkle in his eye, Santa grinned again. "See you to-morrow at the farm," he said as he turned to leave. When he reached the door, Santa shouted, "Let me know if you need anything, Tinker."

"Oh, I think I have everything now, sir," Tinker teased.

The warmth of Santa's laughter filled the room as an all-over-tickled grin seemed to sweep through Tinker.

When Father Chris returned with the special lamp and runner, he could not help but notice something different about Tinker. The young elf appeared to almost glow. When he commented on it, Tinker simply said, "Santa was just here."

Father Chris chuckled, "Well, that'll do it." Placing the special lamp upon the table, Father Chris said, "This was last on your list. Is there anything else I can do?"

Tinker thought for a moment, "It's just a matter of attaching everything now and testing it," he said. "Why don't you go on home? This is going to take a little while." With an impish grin, Tinker added, "I just need to 'tinker' with it."

"Seems to me you need a break," Father Chris teased. Placing a lunch basket, on top of the drawing table, he said, "Pixie sent this. She said Mathias helped her fix it, so I would say it's anybody's guess as to what's in there."

Tinker laughed. "Probably a lot of fruit."

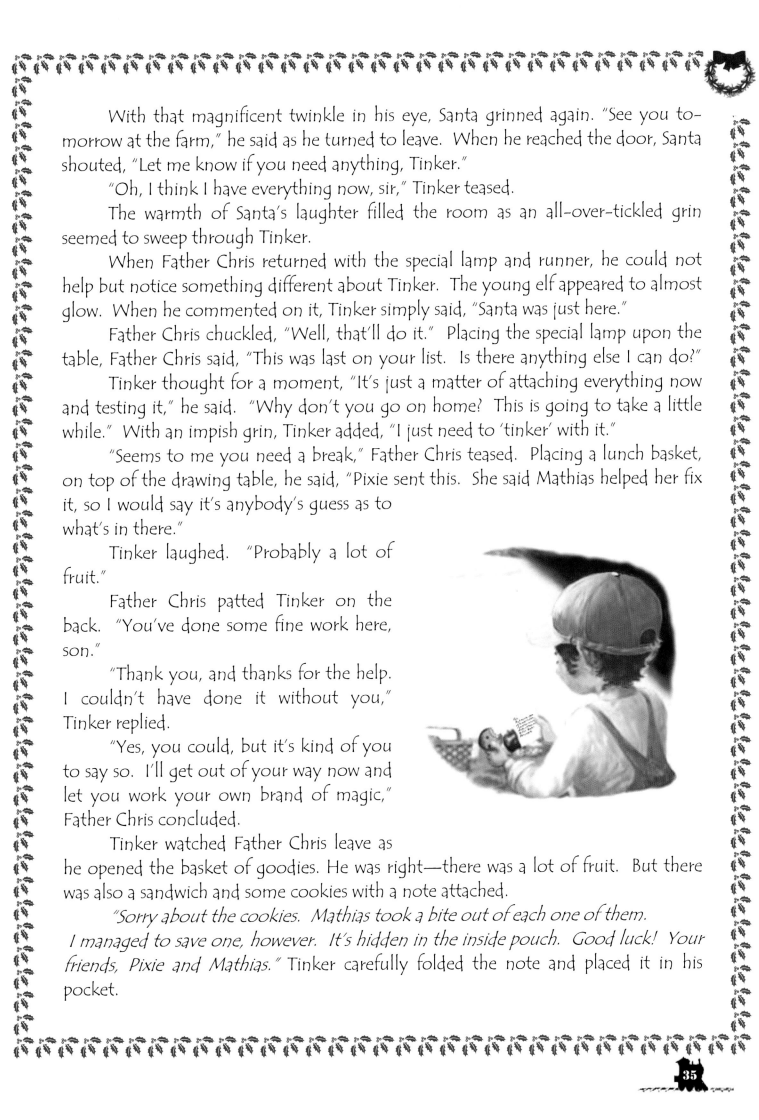

Father Chris patted Tinker on the back. "You've done some fine work here, son."

"Thank you, and thanks for the help. I couldn't have done it without you," Tinker replied.

"Yes, you could, but it's kind of you to say so. I'll get out of your way now and let you work your own brand of magic," Father Chris concluded.

Tinker watched Father Chris leave as he opened the basket of goodies. He was right—there was a lot of fruit. But there was also a sandwich and some cookies with a note attached.

"*Sorry about the cookies. Mathias took a bite out of each one of them. I managed to save one, however. It's hidden in the inside pouch. Good luck! Your friends, Pixie and Mathias.*" Tinker carefully folded the note and placed it in his pocket.

The next day after "Ah-Choo's" morning run, Father Chris, Tinker, Santa, Pixie, and Mathias, who was hidden in a basket, chugged out to the deserted farm.

About three hundred feet from the farm, Father Chris stopped the train, and he and Pixie got off. Tinker, who had been helping Mathias shovel coal, stepped behind the controls. Santa stood beside Tinker, and Mathias ran back and forth from the tinder to the firebox with his small shovel, sometimes filled and sometimes not.

Placing his hand on Tinker's shoulder, Santa said, "Just tell me when you're ready, son."

Tinker studied the steam gauge. After a few moments, he nodded, "Now, sir."

Santa placed his finger aside his nose. Suddenly, with a shimmy and a shake and a jerk forward, the front of that old engine rose and gently left the ground.

Father Chris shook his head in disbelief. Pixie squealed with delight. Tinker yelped, Mathias patted the top of his head, and Santa simply smiled.

Way up in the balmy, lavender blue sky was old Engine No. 25. Miraculously that awkward duckling of a train became a smooth sailing swan. High above the hilltops, "Ah-Choo" flew as she sailed across that blue sky like a beautiful bird in fanciful flight. With a ribbon of steam trailing behind them, the little group flew with the grace of a glider around the forsaken farm. They flew high, low, and in-between. They made circles, loops, and figure eights. They flew across meadows, over hills, and between trees. Truly, it was breathtaking to see! Father Chris and Pixie watched in awe.

When it came time to land, Santa suggested they try the barn first since it was largest. Tinker agreed. They made one more loop around the farm, and Tinker studied the roof of the barn carefully as they flew past. As he prepared the train for landing, Tinker instructed Mathias to stop shoveling coal and fasten his seatbelt. Pixie had worked with Mathias, and the little chimp followed his orders like a well-trained cadet.

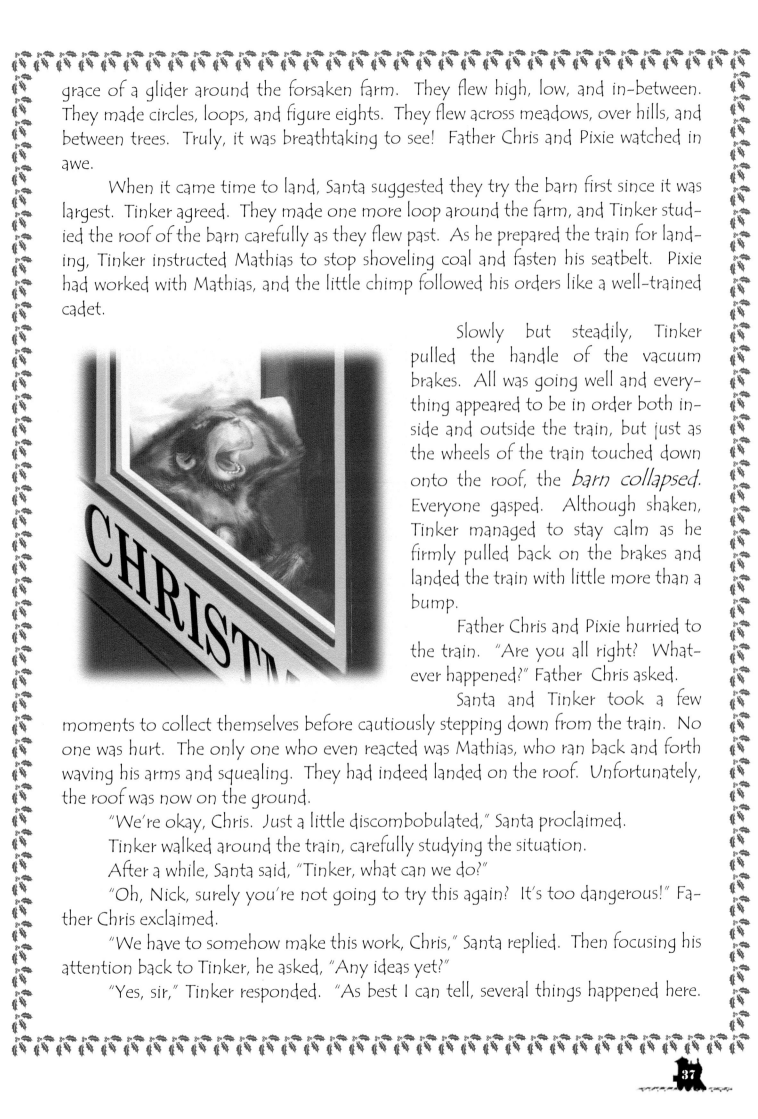

Slowly but steadily, Tinker pulled the handle of the vacuum brakes. All was going well and everything appeared to be in order both inside and outside the train, but just as the wheels of the train touched down onto the roof, the *barn collapsed*. Everyone gasped. Although shaken, Tinker managed to stay calm as he firmly pulled back on the brakes and landed the train with little more than a bump.

Father Chris and Pixie hurried to the train. "Are you all right? Whatever happened?" Father Chris asked.

Santa and Tinker took a few moments to collect themselves before cautiously stepping down from the train. No one was hurt. The only one who even reacted was Mathias, who ran back and forth waving his arms and squealing. They had indeed landed on the roof. Unfortunately, the roof was now on the ground.

"We're okay, Chris. Just a little discombobulated," Santa proclaimed.

Tinker walked around the train, carefully studying the situation.

After a while, Santa said, "Tinker, what can we do?"

"Oh, Nick, surely you're not going to try this again? It's too dangerous!" Father Chris exclaimed.

"We have to somehow make this work, Chris," Santa replied. Then focusing his attention back to Tinker, he asked, "Any ideas yet?"

"Yes, sir," Tinker responded. "As best I can tell, several things happened here.

Look at the rafters on the barn. The wood is rotted. The rafters probably couldn't have held up the sleigh either. But I also think I can cushion the brakes a little more by applying more compressed air to the cylinders leading to the brake shoes. And if I come in parallel to the roof instead of at an angle, that should help. I think those adjustments will solve the problem."

Santa studied Tinker's eyes for a moment. "Then we can try again tomorrow?"

"I believe so, sir," Tinker answered.

"Good. Tomorrow it is then," Santa announced.

As they were returning to Christmas Village, Santa patted Mathias on the head, and said, "You did a good job, my little friend." Mathias screeched, and Santa replied, "I take it then that you agree?"

Everyone joined in the laughter, as the concern over the job that lay ahead of them weighed heavily on each of their hearts and minds. Venting some of the steam caused by that concern was a welcome relief.

# Chapter Seven

# Landing Lightly

The next day all gathered at the appointed time to practice their mission. Tinker appeared to have no problems in either taking off or flying "Ah-Choo." With Santa at his side, Tinker flew the old engine through the air with great ease like an experienced pilot-engineer. Everyone cheered! But when it came time to land, concern surfaced across each and every face.

Father Chris stood soundly on the ground, watching, waving, smiling outwardly, praying inwardly. Pixie stood next to him, her small hands clasped together.

While he carefully guided "Ah-Choo," Tinker prayed a silent prayer as they made one last, slow circle around the farm. As he maneuvered the old engine to land parallel to the roof, Tinker slowly applied the newly cushioned brakes. Swooshing sounds pierced the quiet as the compressed air pushed against the brake cylinders. As pressure from the pistons engaged the brake shoes, the large runner touched down onto the roof without so much as a thump. Tinker had eased "Ah-Choo" onto the top of that farmhouse like a butterfly landing on a flower. With little more than the slight chunk of a bump when the tinder touched, everything had gone perfectly.

Everyone jumped for joy, especially Mathias. The little chimp was so excited that he jumped into Tinker's arms. When everyone laughed, Mathias not only began patting the top of his own head, he patted the top of Tinker's also. Delighted with their success and with Mathias hanging onto Tinker's neck, the train-flying trio climbed down the trellis of the old farmhouse.

"Good job, son. Very good job!" Santa said as he shook Tinker's hand.

Father Chris and Pixie ran over to greet them. "Fantastic job, Tinker!" Father Chris exclaimed. "Mighty fine landing! None better. You truly are a wonder, son!"

"Oh, Tinker, you were wonderful, just wonderful!" Pixie praised.

Tinker blushed, dropped his head, and simply said, "Thank you."

After more excited talk and planning about the next few days, Pixie turned to Santa. "What about me? When do I get to practice with Mathias on the train?"

A look of concern crossed Father Chris's face. Santa recognized the look and gently asked, "How about a practice run tomorrow? Like a dress rehearsal." Placing his hand on Father Chris's shoulder, he added, "That okay with you, Chris?"

Father Chris tried to swallow the lump that had formed in his throat. After a moment, he nodded his head in agreement. "Yes, we can do that."

"We'll meet at the same time tomorrow then," Santa concurred.

Pixie took her uncle's hand. "It'll be okay, Uncle Chris. You said yourself, I'll be in the best of hands."

Father Chris bent over and kissed the top of Pixie's head. "I know that, dear. It's just hard to let go sometimes. You go as the child of my heart and return all grown up."

Pixie hugged her uncle in sweet appreciation. "I hope I will always be the child of your heart just as you will always be the beloved uncle of mine."

Father Chris tweaked Pixie's nose. "Must you always be so wise?" he chided.

Tinker climbed back onto the roof of the . Waiting for the signal from Santa, he gently guided the train down from the rfarmhouse and into the trainoof. As he pulled "Ah-Choo" to a stop, Santa, Father Chris, and Pixie, with Mathias in her arms, climbed aboard. Hovering just above the ground, Tinker guided the train north towards the rail-road tracks.

"Good work, son!" Santa said. "Tomorrow we have our dress rehearsal," he added.

# Chapter Eight

# Practicing with Pixie

Santa, Father Chris, Pixie, Tinker and Mathias met at the farm the next day for their dress rehearsal. One of the best parts for Tinker was practicing with Pixie. He was smitten for sure. Pixie was sweet and kind, and she believed in him. And for the first time, Tinker felt special.

As soon as Pixie was given a shovel, Mathias quickly grabbed his shovel and began shoveling coal.

"I thought I was supposed to train you," Pixie giggled. Turning to Santa, she teased, "I know I don't have any job experience, but I never thought training for my first job would come from a chimp."

"Your greater talents require no training, Pixie," Santa acknowledged.

Father Chris watched the little troop from the ground and prayed.

All went well, as each practiced his or her appointed job, and each time Tinker landed "Ah-Choo" like an experienced pilot-engineer.

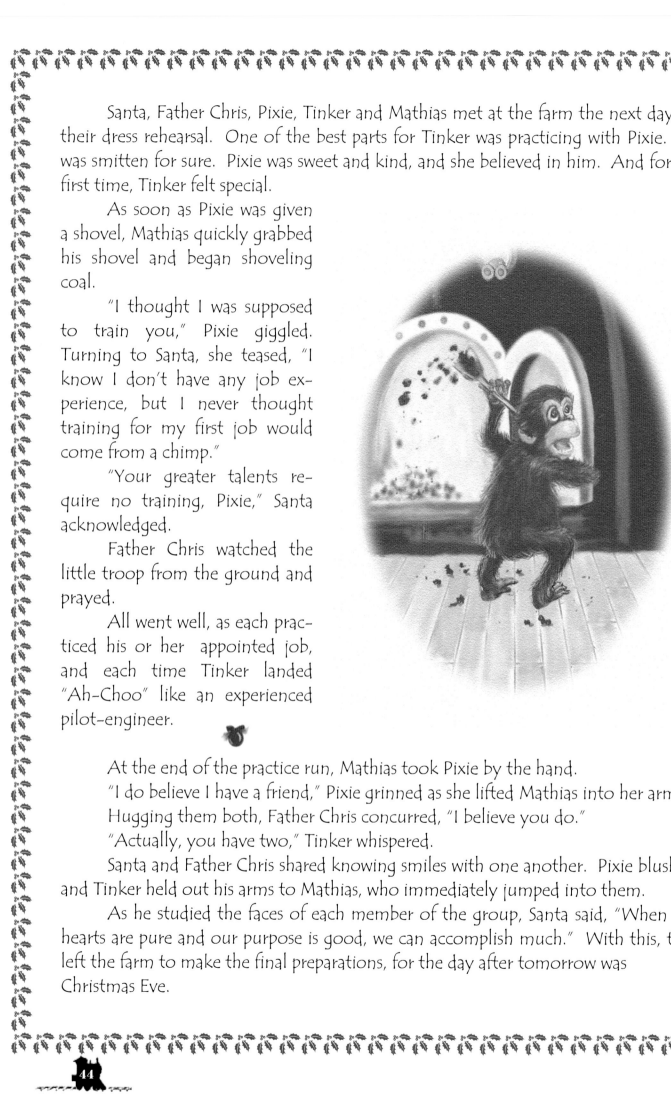

At the end of the practice run, Mathias took Pixie by the hand.

"I do believe I have a friend," Pixie grinned as she lifted Mathias into her arms.

Hugging them both, Father Chris concurred, "I believe you do."

"Actually, you have two," Tinker whispered.

Santa and Father Chris shared knowing smiles with one another. Pixie blushed, and Tinker held out his arms to Mathias, who immediately jumped into them.

As he studied the faces of each member of the group, Santa said, "When our hearts are pure and our purpose is good, we can accomplish much." With this, they left the farm to make the final preparations, for the day after tomorrow was Christmas Eve.

All had gone so well that day that Tinker's small body appeared to swell with all the happiness he felt, but Tinker's happiness soon turned to anguish. Everyone in the Village seemed to know about what had happened when Tinker had tried to land the train onto the roof of the old barn. And once again Tinker found himself the brunt of everyone's cruel jokes.

One of the elves had apparently overheard Santa telling Mrs. Claus what had happened at the barn, and the eavesdropping elf had wasted no time sharing this Tinker-tale with other elves, who also shared it.

Santa knew none of this. The elves never teased Tinker in front of Santa, for they knew Santa frowned upon unkind behavior of any sort.

Prior to this moment, Tinker had been happy in his heart with his train-landing accomplishments. He would have liked nothing more than to have been able to enjoy the company of the other elves and share his joy. But Tinker went home alone with only Mathias to keep him company.

The next two days Tinker worked very hard preparing Engine "Ah-Choo," Mathias, and himself for their long journey. He made sure the tinder was stocked with plenty of coal and the boiler with plenty of water, checked locations where they might refill along their journey, packed fruit treats for Mathias, and had his best uniform cleaned for the trip. A special place inside the train had to be prepared for all the toys.  When this was done, Tinker helped out in the Production Department so that all Christmas requests could be filled.

To Tinker, these days were busy days, but good days.  Tinker liked to work, and besides, the teasing didn't bother him so much when he was busy.  Christmas was special and for him, this Christmas was even more so.  Tinker vowed to allow nothing to diminish the beauty and wonder of it.

# Chapter Nine

# Oh, Special of Special Days!

On Christmas Eve, Tinker met Santa at the appointed time. Tinker had engineered "Ah-Choo" to Sleigh-Side Manor early in order for the elves to load the precious goods that would be carried to children everywhere. Mathias had remained the only secret left intact, but soon everyone would know. It had been decided that Pixie should bring Mathias to the Manor, as the other elves would be less likely to tease her.

Uriah, like the other elves, had heard of the barn roof fiasco and had already spoken to Santa about it. Although Santa might be assured that the accident was a one-time incident, Uriah was not so certain since Tinker was involved.

Uriah supervised with precision and care. He took pride in his work, and he did a good job. But he did not like surprises or changes in procedure. Like the others, Uriah did not know about Mathias, and undoubtedly he would not be pleased.

When Pixie arrived with the little chimp on her arm and began to help him aboard the train, Uriah bellowed out, "What is this?"

The sound of Uriah's deep, loud voice frightened Mathias so that he ran and hid underneath his seat and refused to come out as long as Uriah was around.

In order that Mathias might be coaxed from underneath the seat, Father Chris gently guided Uriah away from the train. "The chimp is quite good," Father Chris said as he took Uriah by the arm. "As a matter of fact, he's so good that if we're not careful, he may put us out of a job," Father Chris teased.

Santa, who had just bid Mrs. Claus farewell, approached the two elves. "He's right, Uriah," Santa said. "If I don't stay on my toes, Mathias may soon have my job!"

With that, everyone laughed.

Looking from Santa to Father Chris and back to Santa, Uriah suspiciously studied the situation. Although his instincts told him otherwise, Uriah felt that he had no choice but to accept their explanation. He breathed a long sigh of frustration and shook his head.

Santa smiled and patted Uriah on the back before climbing aboard. With the little chimp in his arms, Santa stood on the top step of the train. Like snowflakes, silence fell across the group as all the elves focused their attention towards Santa. In that soft voice that comes from the heart, Santa said, "My friends, my small friend here goes by the name of Mathias. He is Tinker's friend, as it would appear that few have extended their hand to Tinker. When asked who could help him engineer this train tonight, Mathias was the only possibility Tinker could offer."

With his cheeks glowing a vibrant pink, Tinker dropped his head.

Pixie's heart ached as she glanced at Tinker. As quietly as a fawn in a forest, she moved to Tinker's side. Facing forward with a certain serene look upon her face, Pixie slowly slid her hand down her side and into her pocket where she removed a piece of folded fabric.

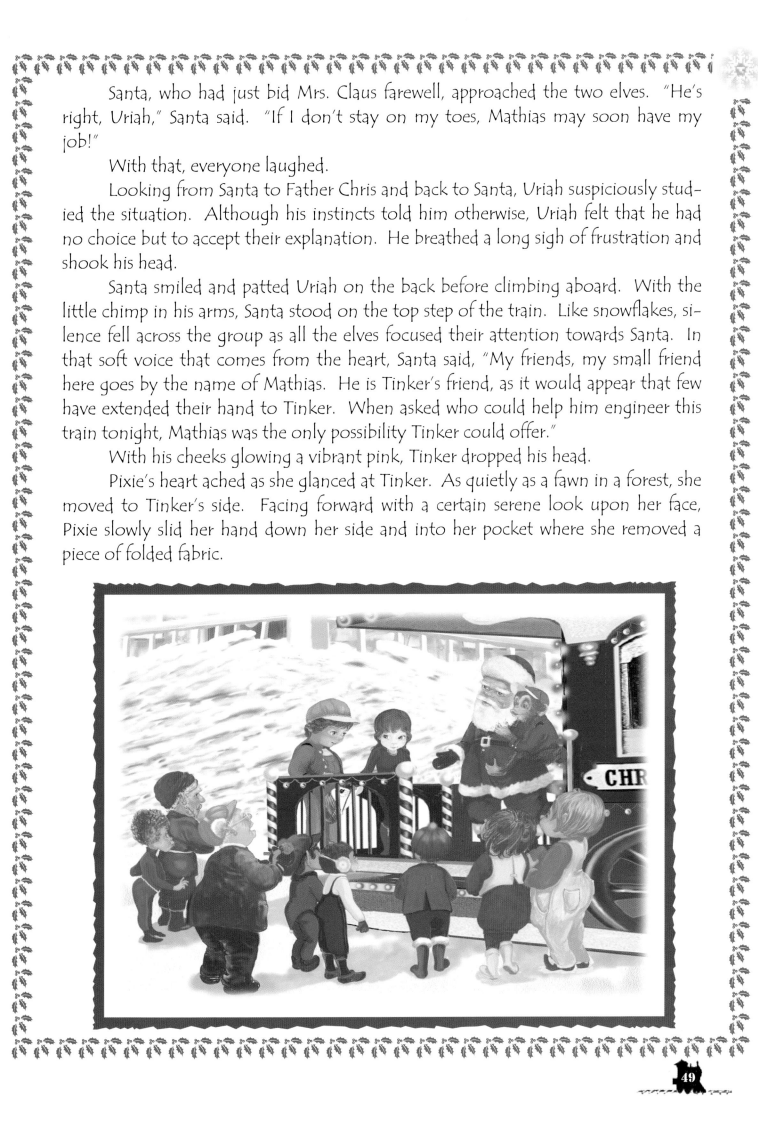

With his head still bowed, Tinker watched Pixie. Her small, delicate fingers moved over and around the fabric until Pixie had unfolded a cap, the shape of which was rather unusual. The cap was made of blue and white-striped denim like an engineer's cap, but the crown was shaped across the top like a pilot's cap. Slowly Pixie slid the cap across to Tinker.

Tinker's eyes opened wide, and a grin spread across his face as he mouthed the words, "For me?"

Pixie's eyes twinkled as she nodded her head.

As Tinker took the cap, he whispered, "Thank you."

Sensing movement behind him, Santa turned, smiled and added, "Father Chris's lovely niece, Pixie, volunteered to help, also, and her efforts have been extraordinary." Again, Santa studied the faces of the elves for a moment before continuing. "My dear friends, if we can open our hearts to the world, surely we can open them to each other."

With this comment, looks of shame crossed several of the faces among the crowd. Many hung their heads.

Santa paused for a moment before concluding, "By the grace of God, we go with your prayers and good wishes." Santa turned and handed Mathias to Tinker who placed the little chimp in his position and gave him his shovel.

A subdued and respectful quiet filled the air, covering the crowd like a heavy quilt. With little noise or chatter, the elves continued to load "Ah-Choo" until she was completely brimming over with toys and goodies.

Pixie took her place beside Mathias, and Santa took his place beside Tinker. As Pixie and Mathias began taking turns shoveling coal into the mouth of the old steam engine, Pixie realized her uncle was watching her. She stopped, flashed him a "don't worry" smile, and threw him a kiss.

Father Chris pulled the imaginary kiss out of the air and to his heart. Then he hurriedly checked the sleigh bells tied to the old engine and gave her shiny, gold No. 25 one last polish before take-off.

Santa placed his hand on Tinker's shoulder. "This is a big night for all of us, Tinker. I just want you to know that I am proud of you, son. You've done an exceptional job so far, and I'm sure you'll do nothing less tonight."

Tinker's eyes sparkled. "Thank you, sir," he said. "That means a lot to me." Tinker turned his attention back to the steam gauge and then to the faces of his crew. After a deep breath, he asked, "Okay, are we ready?"

Santa and Pixie both nodded their heads, and Mathias bounced up and down. But just as they were about to leave, Uriah's deep voice rang out, "Tinker, I want to see you and that chimp of yours when you get back. I've got a job for him. That is, if it's all right with you?"

Tinker smiled and gave Uriah an A-okay sign. When Mathias saw this, he jumped into Tinker's arms and gave Uriah an A-okay sign also.

Everyone laughed as Tinker placed Mathias back into position.

Chuckling and shaking his head, Uriah added, "And it's dinner at my house when you get back, too. I want to hear all about this train and this trip 'cause it's sure the wildest thing I've ever seen. And I've seen a lot!"

Everyone laughed again, and several other elves chimed in, "Me, too!" Tinker nodded and grinned. As he pulled the whistle to alert everyone of their departure, all the elves stepped back. All of a sudden, Father Chris stood at attention and saluted Tinker. Not to be outdone, Uriah followed suit. Suddenly all the other elves fell into a sort of haphazard formation and stood at attention also. Together, they all saluted Tinker. For the first time, Tinker felt warmth from people he knew as neighbors. With a sense of purpose, Tinker returned their salute.

Santa stood beside Tinker, pleased and warmed by the sight of his family of elves. Tinker pulled the train whistle, and Santa placed his finger aside his nose. With a lunge forward, Santa, Tinker, and crew took off into the pale-purple wonder of that late afternoon sky. Silver sleigh bells glistened and tingled in the crisp, afternoon air and there against an azure-blue background old Engine No. 25, with her chunky, soot-black body, smoothly sailed away. Like a large, sassy sea serpent, she sailed across that winter sky, a sky that would soon be filled with a million twinkling stars that caught and contained the heartfelt wishes of children everywhere.

"We go in search of rainbows," Santa whispered, "for if a pot of gold lies at one end of a rainbow, it is surely children who lie at the other."

Tinker nodded his head in agreement.

As the wheels turned and the steam engine churned, smoke billowed up, over, and behind the old engine as Pixie and Mathias shoveled coal in take-turn unison. Although Mathias shoveled somewhat playfully at times, he shoveled nonetheless.

And Santa and Tinker plotted their path and planned their journey across what at times seemed to be a never-ending night sky.

When they reached their first house, Tinker held his breath as he said a silent prayer. He had practiced landing both with a full train and with an empty one, on the rooftop of the old farmhouse and on the rooftop of the tool shed. And although Tinker had done an admirable job on each, this time was different. This time there were people inside. If anything went wrong, they could be hurt. It would be nice not to wake them, but Tinker would be happy just to land the train without demolishing their home.

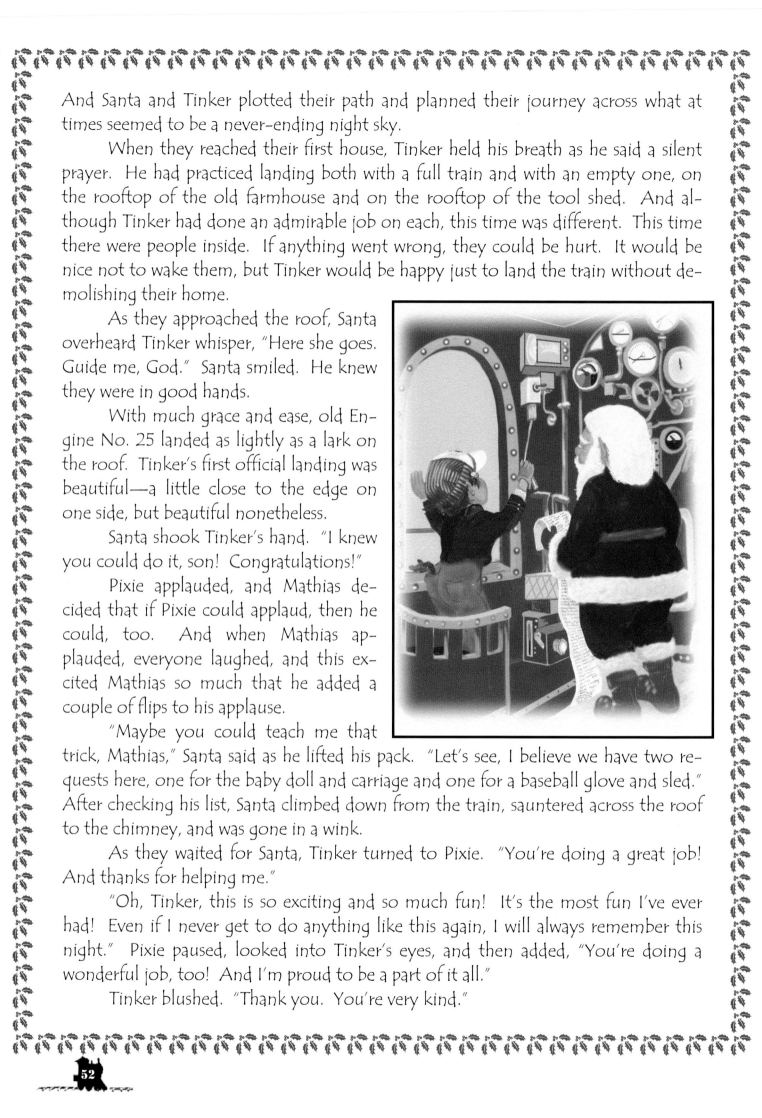

As they approached the roof, Santa overheard Tinker whisper, "Here she goes. Guide me, God." Santa smiled. He knew they were in good hands.

With much grace and ease, old Engine No. 25 landed as lightly as a lark on the roof. Tinker's first official landing was beautiful—a little close to the edge on one side, but beautiful nonetheless.

Santa shook Tinker's hand. "I knew you could do it, son! Congratulations!"

Pixie applauded, and Mathias decided that if Pixie could applaud, then he could, too. And when Mathias applauded, everyone laughed, and this excited Mathias so much that he added a couple of flips to his applause.

"Maybe you could teach me that trick, Mathias," Santa said as he lifted his pack. "Let's see, I believe we have two requests here, one for the baby doll and carriage and one for a baseball glove and sled." After checking his list, Santa climbed down from the train, sauntered across the roof to the chimney, and was gone in a wink.

As they waited for Santa, Tinker turned to Pixie. "You're doing a great job! And thanks for helping me."

"Oh, Tinker, this is so exciting and so much fun! It's the most fun I've ever had! Even if I never get to do anything like this again, I will always remember this night." Pixie paused, looked into Tinker's eyes, and then added, "You're doing a wonderful job, too! And I'm proud to be a part of it all."

Tinker blushed. "Thank you. You're very kind."

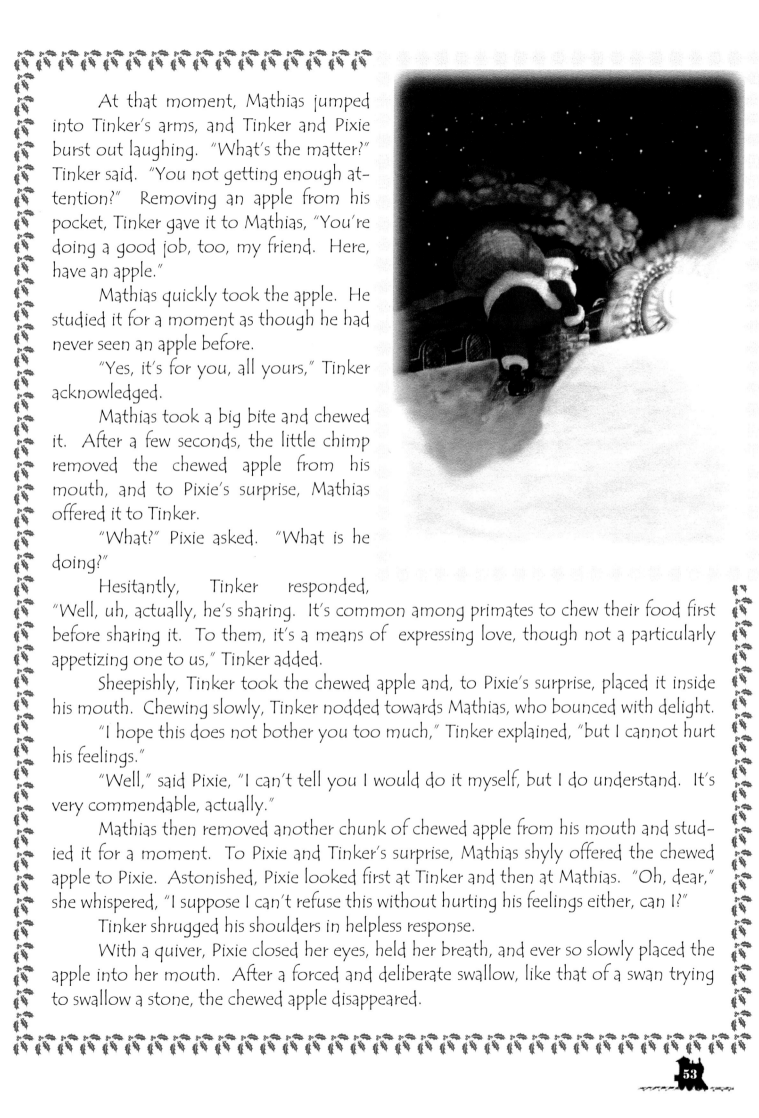

At that moment, Mathias jumped into Tinker's arms, and Tinker and Pixie burst out laughing. "What's the matter?" Tinker said. "You not getting enough attention?" Removing an apple from his pocket, Tinker gave it to Mathias, "You're doing a good job, too, my friend. Here, have an apple."

Mathias quickly took the apple. He studied it for a moment as though he had never seen an apple before.

"Yes, it's for you, all yours," Tinker acknowledged.

Mathias took a big bite and chewed it. After a few seconds, the little chimp removed the chewed apple from his mouth, and to Pixie's surprise, Mathias offered it to Tinker.

"What?" Pixie asked. "What is he doing?"

Hesitantly, Tinker responded, "Well, uh, actually, he's sharing. It's common among primates to chew their food first before sharing it. To them, it's a means of expressing love, though not a particularly appetizing one to us," Tinker added.

Sheepishly, Tinker took the chewed apple and, to Pixie's surprise, placed it inside his mouth. Chewing slowly, Tinker nodded towards Mathias, who bounced with delight.

"I hope this does not bother you too much," Tinker explained, "but I cannot hurt his feelings."

"Well," said Pixie, "I can't tell you I would do it myself, but I do understand. It's very commendable, actually."

Mathias then removed another chunk of chewed apple from his mouth and studied it for a moment. To Pixie and Tinker's surprise, Mathias shyly offered the chewed apple to Pixie. Astonished, Pixie looked first at Tinker and then at Mathias. "Oh, dear," she whispered, "I suppose I can't refuse this without hurting his feelings either, can I?"

Tinker shrugged his shoulders in helpless response.

With a quiver, Pixie closed her eyes, held her breath, and ever so slowly placed the apple into her mouth. After a forced and deliberate swallow, like that of a swan trying to swallow a stone, the chewed apple disappeared.

If Tinker had any doubts about how much of his heart Pixie now possessed, they melted at that moment.

Pixie opened her eyes as a startled look crossed her face. She appeared to be surprised that she had actually survived the ordeal. "Oh, I hope I don't have to do that too often!" Pixie said as she half-laughed and half-shuddered.

Although Tinker tried not to laugh, a muffled chuckle slipped out. "I'm sorry," he said. "He must like you a lot." Tinker paused, lowered his eyes, then softly added, "We both do."

Before Pixie could respond, Santa returned with an empty pack, his work finished at this their first stop. Pixie and Mathias began shoveling coal. Tinker took his place at the controls and looked to Santa. Placing his finger aside his nose, off they rose. And such was their procedure for the rest of the night. All was going so well that they soon found themselves an hour ahead of schedule. Santa was pleased and shared his pleasure by offering kind words of appreciation to all.

As they were returning home, Santa placed his arm around Tinker's shoulders, "Tinker, my friend, no one could have done a better job."

"Thank you, Santa," Tinker replied. "Doing a good job was all I wanted— *with all my heart.*"

"I know, son, and that's exactly how you did it, with all your heart. If you remember that in all you do, it will take you far," Santa added.

"Yes, sir," Tinker said softly.

Happy in their hearts and with their work done, Santa and the train-flying pilot-engineer and crew were on their way home.

# Chapter Ten

# Journey's End

The little Christmas engine had chugged and churned throughout the night until each and every special delivery had been made. When darkness turned to daybreak, the weary travelers turned towards home. As they were coming in for their landing, Tinker's attention was captured by something unusual at Sleigh-Side Manor. Tinker studied the Manor for a moment and then asked, "Santa, what is that on the Manor?"

Santa looked where Tinker indicated. "Well, I'm not sure, son," he said, "but from here, it looks like some sort of sign, a banner maybe."

Upon closer look, they were able to see that it was indeed a banner hung across the rooftop of the Manor. Upon it was painted,

"WELCOME TO SLEIGH-SIDE 'STATION'!
TINKER, YOU'RE OUR HERO! CONGRATULATIONS TO ONE AND ALL!"

As Tinker pulled Engine "Ah-Choo" to a stop at the end of the lane, several elves came running out of the Manor, cheering. Uriah had assembled a small band which was playing "Here Comes Santa Claus."

To their surprise, Uriah suddenly yelled out, "We have another verse!" In his deep, husky voice, Uriah began singing, and the other elves quickly joined in.

Here comes Tinker-elf, here comes Tinker elf,
With Pixie and Santa Claus,
All in a train with a chimpanzee,
That Tinker lands with ease.
Christmas care to all God's own
As we fill our hearts with light
With grace and love from the Lord above,
'Cause Tinker engineers tonight!

The elves stopped singing, and Uriah walked over to Tinker, who had climbed down from the train. With his hand extended, Uriah said, "I'm not much of a song writer Tinker, and apparently I've not been much of a friend. We seem to have forgotten why we're here, and it took Nick to remind us. But we *do* remember, Tinker, and we hope you can find room in your heart to forgive us."

Tinker's grin glowed like a crescent moon and lit up his face as he shook Uriah's hand. With that, Uriah gave Tinker a bear hug, and everyone applauded.

Santa glowed in the goodness that was naturally his, and he and Father Chris exchanged warm looks like knowing parents.

Father Chris extended his arm to Santa as he stepped down from the train, and Santa extended his arms to Mathias, who eagerly jumped into them. All the noise had been somewhat frightening to Mathias, and he gladly clung to Santa.

Pixie waited at the top of the steps of the train. "Tinker," she called softly.

Tinker looked up and felt his heart stir at the sight of her delicate features. "Excuse me, Uriah," Tinker said as he moved towards the train. Smiling sheepishly at Pixie, he extended his hand to her.

When her tiny feet touched the bottom step, Tinker carefully lifted Pixie and lowered her to the ground. Pixie curtsied and then, to Tinker's surprise, leaned forward and kissed him ever so lightly on the cheek.

Tinker blushed fire-engine red.

"Thank you, Tinker. You are very gallant," Pixie said.

Several of the elves bumped elbows and giggled among themselves. Father Chris chuckled, "Tinker, my boy, seems to me you are quite the engineer, far more than Nick and I first realized."

Tinker continued to blush bright red and beautiful just like Rudolph's nose.

Santa nodded in agreement, and in the spirit of the moment, he added, "We only promised to keep her safe, Chris. We're not responsible for matters of the heart."

Mrs. Claus, who had just come to greet Santa and the others, scolded the two teasers. "Now stop that, boys. Don't embarrass them. They make a lovely couple." As she took Santa by the arm, Mrs. Claus said, "We've some hot chocolate and tea cakes inside, dear. You all must be very tired."

Everyone followed Santa and Mrs. Claus to the Manor. Mathias had climbed into Mrs. Claus's arms, and she cuddled and talked to him as they ambled along. The other elves lifted Tinker to their shoulders, chanting, "Here comes Tinker-elf! Here comes Tinker-elf!" Pixie skipped and twirled happily behind them.

Father Chris took a few minutes to absorb all the happenings as the merry group made their way towards the Manor. Removing an oilcloth from his pocket, he carefully polished the glistening gold of the No. 25. "You did a good job, old friend. But then, you were in good hands, weren't you?" As he turned off the special searchlight Tinker had modified to the front of the engine, something on the ground caught his attention. There in the snow was the cap that Pixie had made for Tinker. Apparently it had fallen when Tinker had been hoisted to the elves' shoulders. Smiling to himself, Father Chris removed it from the ground, shook off the snow, and carefully reshaped it. As he contemplated the cap, the old elf spoke softly to himself, "Sometimes we simply believe, sometimes we practice believing, and sometimes we must test our beliefs."

Placing the cap inside his pocket, Father Chris jingled the bells he had previously tied along side the engine. He smiled and shook his head in wonder. Looking in the direction of the Manor, he cited:

"The best gifts come from the heart.
They do not have to be wrapped.
Or come from crafts or fine art.
They come without warning from somewhere inside.
They come as love from God with whom we abide."
Blessed morning to all at this Christmastide."

Father Chris studied the dawn sky.
"It's going to be a good Christmas."

The End